THE FLITHER PICKERS

When Theresa Tomlinson was young she wanted to be a ballerina – not a writer at all. It wasn't until she was a thirty-year-old mother of two that she began to write down the stories she'd made up to entertain her children. She is now the author of several books, including *Riding the Waves* and *Meet Me by the Steelmen*, both of which were shortlisted for the prestigious Carnegie Medal.

In writing *The Flither Pickers*, she drew on her own childhood experiences, as well as certain historical facts, such as the launching by women of the Runswick Bay lifeboat in 1901. The book is set on the north-east coast of England – an area around which Theresa travelled extensively as a small child. The idea for the story came from the photographs of Frank Meadow Sutcliff, on whom the character of the Picture Man is based and whose expressive black and white pictures illustrate this book. Married with three children, Theresa Tomlinson lives in Sheffield.

Theresa Tomlinson

The Flither Pickers

WALKER BOOKS
AND SUBSIDIARIES
LONDON • BOSTON • SYDNEY

First published 1987 by the Littlewood Press
This edition published 1992 by Walker Books Ltd
87 Vauxhall Walk, London SE11 5HJ

10 9 8 7 6 5 4 3

Text © 1987 Theresa Tomlinson
Photographs © The Sutcliffe Gallery, Whitby
Cover illustration © 1990 Anne Yvonne Gilbert

Printed in England by Clays Ltd, St Ives plc

British Library Cataloguing in Publication Data
A catalogue record for this book is available
from the British Library.

ISBN 0-7445-2043-6

Acknowledgements

I have tried to make the details of the fisherwomen's lives as realistic as possible. I have found the following books very useful:

Frank Sutcliffe: Photographer of Whitby by Michael Hiley, published by Gordon Fraser

Frank Meadow Sutcliffe, Photographer: A Selection of His Work compiled by Bill Eglon Shaw, published by the Sutcliffe Gallery

Frank Meadow Sutcliffe: A Second Selection compiled by Bill Eglon Shaw, published by the Sutcliffe Gallery

The Nagars of Runswick Bay by J.S. Johnson, published by Caedmon of Whitby

Mary Linskill: 1840-1891 by Cordelia Stamp, published by Caedmon of Whitby

Mary Linskill: The Whitby Novelist by David Quinlan and Arther F. Humble, published by Horne and Son Ltd

Yorkshire Fisherwomen, an article published by the Spare Rib Co-operative

The Green Howards by Geoffrey Powell, published by Hamish Hamilton

The Publishers wish to thank the Sutcliffe Gallery, 1 Flowergate, Whitby, North Yorkshire, for their helpful advice.

Also by Theresa Tomlinson

Haunted House Blues
Meet Me by the Steelmen
Riding the Waves
The Rope Carrier

Dedicated to the fishing families of the North-East Coast

Author's Note

Although the characters from Sandwick Bay are all fictitious, the idea for the story came from the photographs of Frank Meadow Sutcliffe, the Whitby photographer. The character of the Picture Man is inspired by Frank Sutcliffe, though it is not in any way an accurate portrayal. Similarly, Sutcliffe's photographs, used to illustrate the book, are not to be confused with the fictional characters I have written about.

I have tried to be as accurate as possible, however, about the character of Mary Linskill, the Victorian Whitby writer.

The launching of the lifeboat is based on a real incident. In 1901 the women of Runswick Bay launched the lifeboat with a scratch crew, led by an old coxswain, when all the men were caught out at sea in a storm. In the real incident no life was lost and the old coxswain needed no persuading. The women were invited to Manchester for a dinner and reception in recognition of their bravery.

Chapter One

I bent my head down and pushed slowly forward into the wind, high on Caedmon's Cliff. Down below I could see Mam and the other flither pickers, out on Sneaton scaur.

I waved and she looked up at us. I dragged my hand back sharp. I shouldn't have made her see us. She'd be mad with me for bringing our Billy out, so early and in such a high wind.

Mam ran towards us, then stopped. I could see her face gone white. Something wrong.

"Liza Welford. Get our Billy!"

That was my sister Irene shouting at me. She'd come up behind Mam. I'd forgotten Billy as I waved and now I turned to see him balancing on the curved cliff edge that crumbles a bit each day, with a steep drop down to the rocks.

"Billy," I yelled. He flinched as I caught his hand and dragged him back.

"You devil," I screamed and clouted him over the ear. "You've scared our mam."

He started to howl and pull away but I kept tight hold of him, while I turned to look back down below.

I saw that the women had gathered round a hunched figure; that was Mam. Irene pushed them aside, making a way through. At last Mam got up, her face still white. She kept looking up at us.

"Get him back home, you silly lass," Irene shouted.

Mam picked up her bucket and went back to work, searching out the best limpets.

I pulled our sobbing Billy along, down the steps, over

the causeway, up the staith and back to our cottage.

"I'll be for it 'cause of you," I said. I kept pinching his hand, I was so angry. I pushed him through our doorway, clapping my hand over his mouth.

"Now shut your noise. We mustn't wake Gran, or we'll have Grandpa Welford fretting again."

He looked up at me, silent now, his shoulders shuddering. I took my hand away and pushed my fingers through his curls, fair and soft, like I wished mine were. It was myself I was mad with, not him. I should have taken better care. 'Specially with the family so feared, and Grandma Esther lying in bed sick.

I heard Grandpa Welford's stumping footsteps on the stairs.

"Is that you, our Liza? Fetch a cup of water, will you? Your grandma's wanting to drink."

I took Grandma's favourite blue-flowered china cup from the dresser and carried it out to the pump beyond our yard. Welford's Yard, it's called. My family had lived there for so many years that the cottages that sprang up around had taken our name too.

I jumped as the water splashed over the edge and wasted into the ground. Grandma would have scolded for that.

"Never take it for granted," she'd say. "Good clean spring water we've got. Never waste it. Better water than in any yard in Sandwick Bay."

I carried the cup back inside. A hard cold lump stuck in my throat; it was thinking of my gran that brought that lump. Her fast tongue, her fierce blue eyes, the way she picked up what you were thinking before you'd spoken. Now she lay abed, getting weaker every day.

Old Miriam, the herb woman, had been called first. She'd given Gran potions, but shaken her head. Then Grandpa Welford and Daniel, my dad, had talked together and sent for the new doctor from Whitby. That

"Lucky to have the choice, my lass."

I nodded and sat there silent, gritting my teeth against the tears.

I heard my name called and a commotion down below. The flither pickers were back.

Gran had fallen asleep. I hated myself; I'd made her talk too much. I crept from the room and went to keep our Billy happy and out of the way, rolling his marbles in the corner of the yard.

Irene was there, getting herself ready to start to shell the limpets, or flithers as we call them. Mam always got back later as she walked the long way round, over the bridge, never crossing the causeway with the others.

Irene glowered at me. Now I'd get it.

"You know nowt, our Liza. Don't you ever take Billy up on them cliffs again."

"I caught him back," I said. "I never let him go so I couldn't catch him back."

I thought she was going to hit me, so fierce and white she went, but Mam walked into the yard and stared at us.

"What's up?"

Irene shook her head. "Nowt . . . but I've caught my thumb again."

Mam sat down beside her and I watched as they worked. They shelled the limpets and mussels, caving and skaning, as we say, putting them to soak and swell in buckets of cold water while they cleaned the lines, picking off the little bits of old bait. They set about fixing the shellfish to the sharp hooks, hundreds of hooks to each line, coiling the line carefully in its special basket, or skep, as they worked. An hour it took to bait each line. Strong hands they both had, flicking fast, but scarred hands . . . Irene's worse than Mam's. I remembered what my gran had said: how I was lucky to have the choice.

When they'd finished Mam went off to the bakehouse, taking her dough. Irene took up her knitting, giving me angry looks. She seemed full of sharp looks and sharp words, not like herself at all. I supposed she was upset about Grandma, as we all were in our own ways. Suddenly she got to her feet and thrust her knitting at me.

"None of your sloppy stitches now." Then, clutching at her stomach, she ran off to our privy at the back.

I looked at the gansey growing fast from her needles. My dad was always needing leggins or cap or gansey to keep him from freezing out at sea.

I sat down. I tried to do a row or two, but my fingers were clumsy beside Irene's. Still, it was something I had to learn – our own Sandwick stitches, with the waves and herring-bone, though even our knitting had a nasty side to it, for if my dad should be drowned and his body washed far away, at least with our pattern on his gansey they'd know he was a Sandwick man.

Chapter Two

The tide turned late that afternoon. Dad had been to look at the sea and he'd given my mam the nod. That meant they were off.

Billy and me went down to the beach with Mam and Irene walking in front, both with coiled lines in their skeps balanced on their heads. We went to give a hand pushing the coble out, for we have no other way to launch our boats in Sandwick Bay. Even our heavy lifeboat, the *Francis Welford*, has to be dragged over the sand and pushed right out into the sea.

Aunt Hannah Welford and Mary our cousin were there and we all helped push out my dad and Uncle Frank in our fine coble, *Sneaton Lass*. John Ruswarp was going off in the *Lily Belle* with his younger brother Sam and Mrs Ruswarp was there to push them out.

Their dad had been drowned five years back and John had taken over his father's boat though he were only fifteen at the time. My dad had helped him learn the work. There'd been three great lads all of an age, all learning together. There was John Ruswarp, our Frank and my cousin Ned Welford. Always laughing and teasing they were. They'd carry me on their shoulders and bring me liquorice from Whitby ... now there was only John Ruswarp still in Sandwick Bay.

They'd gone out together one night, all three, though my dad had warned that the sea was too rough. There'd been a storm and my cousin Ned was drowned. Our Frank changed after that; he seemed feared of going out himself. He said it was getting so that the fishing was not worthwhile, what with the new fangled trawlers draining the sea of the fry.

Then the war in South Africa had come and there'd been a call for volunteers. Our Frank went off to Scarborough and joined the Green Howards. My dad was broken-hearted about it. He thought nowt to being a soldier.

"If he thinks it's hard working the boats, he'll find it harder where he's going," he said. Dad never mentioned Frank's name these days, but he picked up all the news he could from South Africa, and lately John Ruswarp had talked about following our Frank.

John was twenty and a handsome-looking fellow, but that day Irene didn't run over to him as she usually did. She didn't even seem to look his way and it was fat Nelly Wright that was hanging round his boat, casting spiteful looks our way and talking at the top of her voice.

We stood on the beach and watched the boats out, then turned back to the village. Mam and Hannah walked up the beach together. Irene and Mary, who were the same age, followed close behind, heads bent together, whispering. They left me out, as though I were a child, left me with Billy tagging at my wet skirts. Mrs Ruswarp came puffing up behind me.

"Here's your friend," she said, pointing up at the staith.

It was her daughter Mary Jane, waving and hallooing, fresh from school.

"Now then Liza, not at school again?" She ran over the shingle and took my arm.

I shook my head. "Y'see I'm not, daft ha'p'orth."

"Is your gran real bad then?"

I nodded and we walked on together.

"Miss Hindmarch was asking after you today, saying that it were a pity if you fell behind."

I shrugged my shoulders. I couldn't care less if I never

went to school again.

"I heard tell," said Mary Jane, "that some of the younger lads at Whitby were wagging off school and the kid-catcher chased them all the way down to the harbour. So they stripped off all their clothes and ran straight into the water."

"They never did."

"Stripped naked they did and kid-catcher, he was furious, but you can be sure he wasn't for getting himself wet. He left them there and turned back into town, looking for others."

"Well, there's a trick," I said.

"Yes, but I've not told you all. Those lads hadn't come out of the water before this picture chap who makes photographs comes staggering down to the front with his boxes and props, and he shouts to them, 'Stay where you are lads and I'll give you a penny.'"

"A penny to share?"

"No, a penny apiece. He set up his photographing things and made a picture of them – there in the water, stripped naked. A penny apiece he gave them and they say they're down there every day since, hoping he'll be back."

"They'd not set kid-catcher on me," I said. "Not this far from Whitby and me a great lass, old enough to be working with me mam."

"No," said Mary Jane. "They'd not bother with a lass, but Miss Hindmarch, she says a lass as clever as you should be at school. Best pupil she thinks you are, and *I* wish you'd come back for I can't work my 'rithmetic without you to help me."

I went to sit with Gran when I got back. Just sat there quiet beside her while she slept. Her breathing was faint, I thought it gone, but then she opened her eyes and took my hand.

"Glad you're here," she said. "Something . . . must tell."

I bent close for her voice was weak.

"William," she said.

"William? You mean our Billy?"

She shook her head and tried again. "William Archer."

I'd not heard of William Archer, but Archer was a name I knew well enough. It was Mam's name before she was married.

"She called . . . she called Billy after him."

"Don't talk now Gran. Rest."

"No," she said, all agitated. "Must tell. I was there, I saw. She's feared . . . more than you know."

Her breath came difficult. I lifted the cup to her lips and helped her drink. She lay back on the pillows, her mouth working soundlessly.

"Rest Gran," I said. "Tell me in the morning and I'll listen well," but she was already asleep, exhausted with her effort.

It was late that night that I was woken from a deep sleep. Mam was shaking me. "Get up lass and fetch Miriam, for your gran is took real bad."

I got up from the mattress that I shared with Irene, knuckling the sleep from my eyes. Mam wrapped my shawl around me and pushed me to the ladder that led down from our loft. I stumbled down our stairs, my heart thudding, and out onto the top staith, down to Miriam's cottage.

She opened quickly to my knocking. "So it's time." There was no surprise. She picked up her basket and followed me.

Gran died in the early hours. Miriam sent us downstairs while she did the laying out. I sat at our kitchen table and couldn't stop shaking. Irene put her arms around me, hugging me close . . . my kind big sister again.

Mam kept calling up the stairs where Grandpa sat. He wouldn't move from the top step, not for all Mam's persuading. He sat up there with his head in his hands and wouldn't come down.

I hated that black bonnet; it smelt of lavender and death.
"You'll wear it for respect," said Mam.
Black silk it was, made in our special Sandwick way from a yard of silk with five pleats measured across the top and a double frill round the bottom. The frill was supposed to stop the water from the fish baskets dripping on your neck, but nobody would carry fish on a black silk bonnet. It was special, for funerals, and we had plenty of them. I shook it out and tied it beneath my chin, swallowing hard.
"I'll wear it for Gran," I said.

Daniel, my dad, missed the tide for two days. When he returned from the sea and found his mother dead, he sat by the fire and wept.
Mam hadn't cried; I don't think she'd found time for there'd been so much to do. Irene was quiet, shut off in a world of her own, but she'd roused herself to go out with me and Mary, bidding our relations and neighbours to come to the funeral. That's always the job of young women in our bay.
Grandpa was the one we all worried about. Such a fine man my grandpa was, real respected in our community. He'd been the lifeboat cox like his father Francis, who our lifeboat's named for. Grandpa has saved so many lives, taking out our heavy boat that's so difficult to launch. Folk still talk about the day that Grandpa went out three times in that dreadful storm that sank the Whitby lifeboat. Our boat survived, though the crew exhausted themselves and one man died of pneumonia. Grandpa's leg was crushed; he's dragged it ever since. My grandpa, who was our hero, wouldn't speak to anyone after Grandma's death. He

shrank into himself . . . shrunk small and grey and lost.

I'd got no tears but I knew they were there, welling up tight inside. After the funeral Irene walked off with John Ruswarp, who'd been waiting for her outside the church. I was surprised Mam didn't call her back to help with the funeral dinner. So it was me who did most of the helping. I did my best and worked hard to see that all our guests got plenty, for it was part of showing respect for the dead one, giving a good feast after the service. But when the plates were cleared and the talking and drinking began, I slipped away.

I went down to the beach, for I knew I'd have a good cry and I didn't want them to see. I sat on Plosher Rock, as Mary Jane and me call it, after the big five-man cobles that go from Whitby Harbour. I pulled the silk bonnet from my head and held it on my lap as I stared out to sea. The tears came slow and choking at first, then pouring freely, bringing relief. I picked up the bonnet from my lap and set it carefully on the dry rock. I'd be in trouble if I soaked it, for it must be wrapped up with lavender and put away for the next.

It was only as calm came that I thought of the night that she'd died and remembered with a sudden catch of breath that she'd wished to tell me something . . . something about young William Archer.

Chapter Three

It was all quiet when I got back and I found Irene standing at the table in the corner of the yard, back in her working dress and apron. She saw my red eyes and swollen face.

"You must put it behind you, lass," she said, quite kind. "Go change your dress; there's a line needs mucking. Dad's gone to rest, for he must go with the tide tonight."

I changed my clothes and went to help. Irene was talkative but I could see that she was still upset. Hannah and Mary had brought bait for us early that morning and we'd the worst job to do now, for we'd baited lines that Dad had not been able to use, so the bait had gone foul. Mucking we called it, and a muckier job there never could be. We hated mucking but it had to be done. Irene's hands shook as she pulled the scraps of stinking bait from the barbs, working slow, for her. I looked from her hands to her face, and she caught that glance. She dropped the line and lifted the backs of her hands to her eyes. Quiet tears ran down her cheeks, tears that she couldn't wipe for her hands were slimed with mouldy bait.

I was shocked. I couldn't think when I'd last seen her cry.

"Is it Gran?"

She shook her head. "Not just Gran. You'll know soon enough . . . so I'll say now. I'm to have a child."

I blinked. I couldn't believe what she was saying.

"Aye, you'll be shocked," she said. "But you don't know yet how strong it can be, that feeling . . . that feeling when you're sweet on a lad."

I couldn't think what to say and she wiped her hands on

her torn apron, searching for a clean corner to dry her eyes.

"Is . . . is it John Ruswarp?"

"Aye, him. Him who wants to be joining the Army, wants to be off fighting, so far away."

I pulled myself together then. I remembered how she'd been sick and running to the privy.

"I should have known," I said. "I should have guessed, a great girl like me. I've thought of nothing but Gran."

"Nay, how should you know such things? You're nobbut a bairn and you stay that way, our Liza."

I went and put my arms round her, hugging her tight, frightened for her.

"I fear 'tis the worst to come," she said. "Mam knows and she's to tell Dad."

"What does Mam say?"

"She says I'm a fool, but I'm not the first and she'll take my side. Best get Dad told, she says, even though he's so sad for Gran. Best get our troubles over, though I dread what he'll have to say."

We stood there quiet, but then Irene seemed to brace herself.

"Now then, our Liza, this won't do. We're forgetting the lines. We must get these done or we'll have trouble indeed."

We returned to our work, but it was different. She was working slow, her hands shaking still, and I worked really hard for once, trying to take the lead. I took the line.

"I'll coil," I said, flicking the baited hooks aside as carefully as I could, thinking that I must learn to do this better. Irene'd find it hard in the coming months. They'll be needing me, I thought.

We finished the lines and Mam went upstairs to wake Dad for the tide and we heard him shouting.

"She's told him," said Irene, her eyes filling with tears.

When Mam came down she sent us both out with Billy.

"Away with you," she said. "Take Billy away up to the heather. Hannah and Mary'll help get them off. He'll be different in the morning. He likes John Ruswarp more than most."

We walked up the hillside, past the old chapel, Billy running ahead. I felt strange with Irene, as though she were someone I didn't really know. I was scared for her, but pleased that she'd told me so much. Treating me like a woman for once. I couldn't help thinking about her and John Ruswarp, what they must have done . . . up there on the hillside, I guessed, where all the couples walk in summer. I knew about that – well, some of the girls at school talked about nothing else. I thought it sounded horrible and I told Mary Jane that I wasn't ever going to let any man do that to me.

I kept thinking about Irene having a bairn, too. I'd be real frightened of that; that was another thing they talked about at school. I couldn't forget how Rachel Danby had told how her sister had screamed so loud they'd all been sent out into the yard and they could still hear her screaming from there.

I remembered our Billy being born. It had been a long and difficult birth, but I never heard a scream or any sound from Mam, though I'd been at home all the time. I was sitting on Grandpa's knee, sniffing at his pipe and poking fresh tobacco into it, when Grandma Esther came to tell us that Billy was born.

Even though I was so small I knew that Mam was very poorly for a long time afterwards and Miriam had said that there'd be no more bairns for Mam.

Now it was going to happen to Irene and she didn't seem to be worrying about that part of it. She was just unhappy about what Dad would have to say and John wanting to go off to join the fighting.

She told me that John wanted them to be wed. He'd

17

always wanted that, but he still wished to go off to South Africa like Frank. He wanted to make something of himself . . . so he said.

We sat down near the bank top where the heather begins, watching Billy jumping and hiding in thick purple clumps. We pulled our shawls tight, for though there was a bright sun, we were well into autumn and a chilly wind blew.

"That Nelly Wright," said Irene. "She'll have something to say when she hears. Such a wag-tongued gossip she is and she's sweet on John herself. She'll be mouthing it all the way to Whitby, she will."

"Nay," I said. "Who cares what fat Nelly says? She'd better not say owt about my sister when I'm there."

Irene smiled and squeezed my hand. "You're a grand sister, our Liza," she said.

Irene had brought her knitting for no time should be wasted and Irene could knit without looking at her hands. She stared out across the bay, her fingers working of their own accord. She was a fine young woman and I could see why John might think her bonny. Even in her working clothes she looked good, with her pink cheeks and clear skin and her hair done in the new fashion that she took such trouble with, curling her fringe in rags each week. She had a little plaited bun at the back and a thick fringe brushed forwards in shiny brown curls, like the new Queen Alexandra. Irene's hair was the same colour as mine. It was only Billy who'd got the fair curls we both wanted.

I asked Irene about William Archer. I told her how Gran had wanted me to know. I wouldn't have asked her before, but she seemed so much more my friend that day.

"Do you know owt of a William Archer?"

"Do you mean that little lad who was Mam's brother?"

"Ah, that must be him," I said. "Gran wanted to tell me

about him, but it was the night she died. She never got it said and I didn't know what she meant."

"I don't know much about him," said Irene. "Just that he was drowned and Mam was with him and it upset her so much that she'll not cross the causeway. That's why she goes the long way round."

"Gran was telling me that I should take more notice of Mam. Gran was always telling me that."

"Aye, so you should. There's not every mother would take her daughter's side, like Mam is with me. Aunt Hannah would know about that little lad William, though. Her and Mam have always been close. I dare say Aunt Hannah would have been there at the time."

We were silent for a while, Billy still happily playing in the heather behind us.

"There they go," I said, pointing down to the beach. We couldn't see very clear, but we could tell which was our boat, the *Sneaton Lass*, and could see Mam and Dad, both with skeps on their heads. We saw John Ruswarp go down with his mam and it looked like Mary Jane with them. She'd not been to school because of the funeral.

Dad went over to John, but we couldn't tell what went on. Time passed and they were still together on the beach, though the other cobles were out. Irene's knitting went faster and faster.

"Oh dear," she said. "There's a to-do, I know there is. Would Dad hit him, do you think?"

"Nay," I said. "John's that much bigger than Dad."

Irene laughed and I joined in. We giggled together, but Irene laughed on after I'd stopped . . . wild laughing, then suddenly it turned to desperate sobbing that frightened me. I put my arms round her and Billy came to stare at us. I didn't know what to do. I thought of Grandma Esther and missed her bitterly. She'd have known what to say and what to do.

"It's all right," said Irene, pushing me away and smiling

wet-faced at Billy. "It's all right, our Billy," she said, pulling him onto her knee while I fished around for the knitting she'd dropped, trying to save the stitches.

We sat on, staring down at the jumbled red roofs of our village. The cottages are crammed tight together on the steep bankside, so that kitchens often overlook their neighbours' bedroom window and we all know each other's business . . . it can't be helped. We sat silent, watching the smoke puthering out of the chimneys and the washing flapping on the lines.

At last we saw that John had gone off in his boat and Dad and Uncle Frank were following.

"Now then, our Billy," said Irene, "it's time we got you home."

Mam was laying out left-overs from the funeral dinner when we got back.

"Good," she said. "You're here. You can eat up these bits for your suppers. Go wash your hands Billy, then sit up at the table."

I couldn't believe it was only that morning that we'd been in our funeral clothes; so much had happened that day. Irene and I stood silent, not knowing how to put the question.

"Now don't stand there like ninnies. Get set down."

"But Mam," said Irene. "What's been said?"

"It wasn't so much saying as shouting," said Mam, "but that's for the best, I think. It was Mrs Ruswarp I was sorry for, her knowing nowt about it and she was so shamed when she realised. Hannah and I walked back with her, though, and told her all and I think she feels better now. Mary Jane was listening too, her eyes wide and her ears flapping. I've never seen John so eager to be off, shouting at his mother and her not understanding. Their Sam knew what was up all right.

"Never mind . . . I think it's over. He'll have calmed down, will your dad, by the time he's had a night out there. So get yourselves set down and make the most of a decent meal. Your gran wouldn't like to see it wasted."

Chapter Four

Dad waited for John on the top staith when he got back the next morning. Mam had been right. They sat together for a while talking quiet and friendly.

When Dad got back to our cottage, he kissed Irene and hugged her and told her she was a silly lass. He'd talked to Uncle Frank while he was out and thought a lot about Esther, his mam, and he'd come to think that it was fine, that a new life should be coming when one so loved had just gone. He said he'd rather she married John Ruswarp than any other, though she could have waited for chapel first. Still, we'd make the best of it and he'd talk to John about the Army and try to get him to change his mind and stay.

I met Mary Jane down on the beach and we went arm in arm to our special rock. Mary Jane was full of it.

"Well fancy our John and your Irene! Fancy them going and doing that. I couldn't believe my ears when I heard all that shouting going on. Eeeh, your dad was vexed, and the whole village heard about it. Weren't you surprised?"

"Well . . . our Irene had told me," I said. "So I knew there'd be a to-do."

"I'll like to be the auntie though," said Mary Jane.

"But it's me as will be the auntie."

"Oh . . ." said Mary Jane, frowning with working it out. "So you will, for Irene's your sister, but John's my brother so I'll be the auntie, too."

"We'll both be aunties," I said. "Both aunties to the same bairn. That makes us like relations, you and me."

We liked the thought of that and we sat there planning the things we'd do. The best aunties in the world we would be.

Along the beach came Nelly Wright and her little gang of friends. Older than us they were and all of them had been bait-gatherers for a year or so. Some of the lasses were kind enough if you saw them by themselves or with their mams, but when they all got together with Nelly Wright as ringleader, a real rough noisy lot they were.

"I've not seen your Irene today," Nelly shouted. "I hear she's got the belly ache, the belly ache that don't go away."

They all shrieked with laughter and shoved at each other with their elbows.

I jumped down from my rock so angry I'd forgotten to be scared.

"Don't you speak about my sister. She's better than the lot of you."

They fell about laughing again.

"Can you hear the flither squeaking?" yelled Nelly. Then she pointed at Mary Jane who'd come and thrust her arm through mine. "Aye, and look at that saucy face. Saucy like her brother she is. You wouldn't believe the tales I could tell about that lad . . . though I'm not so low as to let him give me the belly ache."

They slapped each other on the backs, still shaking with their laughing, and turned to walk on up the beach.

I stuck my tongue out at their backs and Mary Jane, she followed behind at a safe distance, holding her skirt out behind her, waving it from side to side, imitating fat Nelly's wobbly walk.

We went back to Plosher Rock, giggling ourselves now. We weren't going to let them spoil us being aunties, whatever they might say.

"I wish our John wouldn't go on about joining the Army though," said Mary Jane. "I can't bear the thought of him going off to the war. He might get himself killed, then the poor bairn'd have no dad."

"Aye," I agreed with her. "I do miss our Frank. It were grand that day when we went over to Scarborough to wave them off." It was such a to-do. Folk were throwing flowers and bands were playing and everyone was singing and shouting. They looked so smart in their uniforms and folk were saying how volunteers had never before gone off like that to fight with the Regulars. It was so lovely, but then suddenly they were gone and we've heard nowt since, only snippets of news that my dad picks up in Whitby and we don't know whether our Frank's alive or dead. We heard that some of the lads came back last August, but never a word have we heard of Frank.

There seemed to be a bit of a commotion up in the village. A group of lads came walking down by the staith following a man, a gentleman almost, but loaded up with boxes and bits and pieces. The lads were carrying things, too. There were folded sticks and an umbrella with black material draped at the sides.

"Well I never," said Mary Jane. "I do believe it's him."

"Whatever do you mean?"

"It's him . . . the picture man, the one I told you about."

"Oooh . . . are you sure it's him?"

"Who else could it be?"

We watched as they walked along the staith to Old Miriam's cottage. We couldn't hear what was going on, but it was clear enough. He wished to make a picture of Miriam. We could tell how pleased she was, flustered and smiling and brushing down her skirt. It took a long time to get the camera fixed, but the picture man had the lads all quiet and good and running at his beck and call.

Miriam sat up straight and smart, like the squire's lady herself, but the picture man didn't seem to be in any hurry to get his photograph done. He talked on and on to

Miriam, and we'd got a fine view of it all up on our rock. At last, when Miriam picked up her knitting and leaned back in her chair chatting . . . suddenly the picture was being made.

We watched them packing everything up ready to leave and we were just going to get down from our rock to follow the procession of lads when the picture man looked our way. He stopped for a moment and held his hand up to shade his eyes, then he started to walk towards us. Our mouths dropped open; straight towards us he came. Mary Jane looked behind to see if there was someone else . . . but there was no one. We looked at each other scared for there was no doubt but he was coming over to us. I was that shocked it fair took my breath away, but there he was standing before our rock, bowing slightly and lifting his hat, the gang of lads waiting farther back.

"You make a fine picture up there on the rock, young ladies. I'd be pleased to make a picture of you."

We stared, then Mary Jane giggled and I couldn't help it; I was giggling too, looking back at this slim man, quite tall with a kind smile and fine bushy beard.

"Do I have your permission, young ladies?"

We giggled again and nodded. "Can if you like."

Again he took a long time setting his camera up. He talked to us as he worked, asking our names and did we live in the bay.

He set up three spindly legs, fastened together, then fixed his camera box on top. A bit wobbly it looked, balanced on the shingle, and he had the lads looking round for a flat-topped stone to fix beneath the back leg. At last it was fixed, but then he had to move the whole contraption farther back and find another stone. At last he seemed satisfied and stayed beneath the cape saying, "That's good . . . that's good."

He had to bend his long legs to get himself to the right height.

"You can't see much in there, can you?" asked Mary Jane, grown bold.

"I can see you fine young ladies," he said. "I see you fine, but upside-down."

We both laughed at that and the laughing made me cheeky. I leant right over, propping up my head with my hand. "Why should we not sit like this then?"

"You goose," said Mary Jane.

"Stay just like that," came the picture man's voice.

So bursting with sauciness, but frozen still, we had our picture made.

"That's done," he said, appearing from under the cape.

"But that was daft," I said.

"Aye, a bit of fun, but I think a good picture. I'll send a copy for your mothers if you tell me where you live."

We did more than tell him, we walked back up the beach with him and showed him our cottages. He spoke all polite to Mam, treating her like a lady. Mam was all shamed with her apron dirty from the skaning and her hands all slimed.

We walked up the hill with him, helping to carry his boxes . . . up to the pony and trap waiting at the top. He asked us if we went to school and Mary Jane told him how Miss Hindmarch wished me back there.

"Is that not Miss Cicely Hindmarch?" he asked.

"Yes indeed," said Mary Jane.

"I'm acquainted with Miss Hindmarch," he said. "A good teacher and a clever woman. If Miss Hindmarch thinks well of you, you must be a smart girl."

Mary Jane nudged me hard.

"Perhaps you should return to school," he said.

"Nay, learning's got nowt to do with the likes of me."

He looked thoughtful for a moment and I thought I'd been rude, but he smiled and lifted his hat. He loaded up the trap with his boxes and went on his way.

"He never gave us any pennies," said Mary Jane.

Chapter Five

Mam was packing a parcel of fish-heads wrapped in cloth when I got back.

"When you've finished with having your head turned, you can run an errand for me. Take these over to poor Annie Lythe. Tell her I'm sorry it's only the heads."

Poor Annie Lythe, as everyone called her, had lost her husband: drowned at sea, the familiar way. Annie had six children all younger than me and we knew she was having a struggle to raise them, but she managed to keep them out of the workhouse somehow. She took in washing and we all gave what we could to help. It wasn't like charity; it was just 'the right thing to do', for we all knew that the next family orphaned could be ours. Mam usually sent a decent fish. If it was fish-heads for Annie Lythe, then it would be fish-head stew for us. With the bad weather starting, Dad'd not be able to get out every time and we'd be mucking the lines.

Annie's cottage was next to Aunt Hannah's and I saw Hannah and Mary sat out at the back baiting lines as I passed. I remembered how Irene had said that Aunt Hannah was the one to ask if I wanted to know more about William, Mam's young brother. But Aunt Hannah has a bit of a sharp tongue and I hurried on to Annie's.

To find Annie, you had to fight your way through sheets and petticoats and frilly drawers all hanging from lines across the yard. She was turning the poss stick in her dolly tub, her sleeves rolled high and her muscles straining, her small kitchen filled with steam.

"Thank your mam kindly," she said, seeing my parcel.

"'Fraid it's only fish-heads," I told her.

"I know the catches have been bad so it's most kind of her," insisted Annie.

Her two youngest girls came and stood before me, tugging at my skirt.

"Nay, I've got no liquorice today," I said, wishing that I'd saved a bit when Dad brought some from Whitby last week. Their dresses were clean but worn and holed. Annie had little time to spare from her laundry work to see to her own girls' clothes.

"I heard about your Irene's trouble," said Annie. "Tell her that I wish her well, will you? When you know how easy life is lost, you value a new life coming."

I thanked her and said goodbye. It's funny, I thought. Funny how it's often those that has least that manages to be kindest.

I dawdled by Aunt Hannah's door, wanting to speak to her, but I needed my courage for Aunt Hannah won't suffer fools. She's not quiet like our mam; she always has plenty to say.

"Well, Liza," said Hannah when she spied me, "you're here at the right time. Get yourself sat down and coil this line, for Mary's to go to Walter Snaith's to fetch our new skeps. You'll earn yourself a cup of tea then."

At least you didn't need an invitation with Hannah.

I sat and helped, but I couldn't think how to ask what I wanted, till Hannah herself showed me the way.

"You should be getting back to school, Liza," she said. "That'd please your mam, now that poor Esther's gone."

"Why . . . I would," I said, "but with Grandpa taken to his bed, there's none to see to Billy but me."

"Aye, there's some as would have Billy down on the beach while the picking's done, but not Martha."

"Grandma Esther wanted me to know," I said, grabbing at my chance.

"Whatever do you mean? Speak sense, lass. What did Esther want you to know?"

I swallowed hard and tried again. "Esther wanted to tell me about young William Archer, but it was the night she died and she never got it said."

"Aah," said Hannah, quite soft for her. "Esther wanted to tell you that, did she? That's what you're here for. Well, Esther did usually know what's best and we should respect her wishes."

I nodded, uncomfortable, while Hannah inspected me.

"I'm not sure as you shouldn't ask your mam . . . but maybe it's easier for someone else to say. I'll tell you what I can."

"I know William Archer was Mam's young brother," I said. "And I know he was drowned, but then we've all had family drowned haven't we, like . . . "

"Aye, like our Ned. True enough, but it's usually in bad weather or a storm and you dread it, but you half expect it. William Archer, he was drowned on a sunny spring afternoon, the sea as calm as you could wish. We were nearby, but we never saw owt amiss . . . not till it was too late."

"You were there then, Aunt Hannah?"

"Oh aye, I was there." Her face went sad and she spoke so quiet I could hardly believe it was my aunt.

"There was me, Esther and old Mrs Lythe – that's Annie's mother-in-law. There was your mam's mother Katherine Archer, too, and we were all fetching the flithers. I'd just started to help with it and I felt jealous of Martha, your mam, her being that bit younger than me and her still being treated like a child. She was left to splash about near the causeway with little William. She'd been told to take care of him, mind."

It felt strange to think of my mam being a young lass and

having to look to her young brother, like I did for Billy.

"It was Esther who saw it first," said Hannah. "'What's up with your Martha?' she said. Katherine looked . . . well we all looked and there she was lying face-down near the causeway, close to the water's edge and the tide going out, for we'd not been picking long. She wasn't shouting or making any sound, but she was kicking and punching at the sand."

I shuddered when I heard that. I couldn't imagine my mam behaving so odd.

"'She's lost that lad,' said Katherine. 'She's let him run off up the staith.' We wandered over to her. We weren't in any hurry, but when we got close we saw that she was in a right state, slavering and biting at the sand. Katherine went and pulled her to her feet. 'Where's the lad?' she asked. 'Has he run off?' Martha didn't answer, just kept opening and shutting her mouth, but she pointed to the sea. Well, then we did worry. Katherine slapped your mam hard across the face. 'Where's the lad?' she asked again and at last poor Martha spoke. 'In the sea.'"

I'd stopped my work on Mary's line and Aunt Hannah never even noticed, so tense her face had gone.

"We stared out to sea," she said, "but there was nowt and it looked so calm we couldn't believe that the lad was in there. Katherine, she suddenly made up her mind to take no chances. She put down her swill and walked straight into the sea – clothes, boots and all – and once she'd done it we all seemed to think that she was right. We followed her and we looked and looked. We went out as deep as we dared, but we found nothing. Even then we weren't sure. We made Katherine come back in. We told her not to worry, we said he'd come running down the staith before long. We stopped our picking; the men'd have to stay at home that night, for a young lad's life means more than a good catch.

"We took Katherine home and searched the village.

Martha was forgotten. Where she went, I don't know, but it was Miriam who brought her home that night. Nobody held her to blame – it was the sea – but I think she blamed herself and as far as I know your mam has never crossed the causeway since."

"But how had William gone?"

"We've never really known, but drowned he was and his body washed up at Sandsend. We could only think that he must have been caught in one of those currents. You can never trust the sea . . . it takes those it wants."

I sat frozen, staring at my aunt, trying to take in all she'd said. Seeing my mam as a child and her so frightened that she'd near gone mad.

"Esther was right," said Hannah, more her usual self. "It's best that you know. Don't mock your mam when she goes traipsing over the bridge or fussing over Billy, and think how she manages to get herself down on that beach, working to feed you bairns."

I nodded. I was chilled right through and I needed Hannah's hot sweet tea to warm me again, but Hannah wasn't one to let you sit and stew.

"Seeing as you're here and Mary's not back, you can come down to the beach with me and your Uncle Frank. Take that wreath from Mary's peg and get that skep fixed."

My aunt went inside for Uncle Frank and I reached the padded band down and pulled it round my head. I lifted the skep I'd been working on and got it comfortably settled in its place. I was glad to be having a job to do, after what I'd heard, and at least Aunt Hannah treated me like I was useful.

Chapter Six

As the weeks went by and the sun shone lower in the sky, the winds blew cold and our lives settled into the hard pattern that each winter brings. The men had to use the longer lines and go farther out. That meant more bait to be fetched and the weather worse for doing it.

Mam and Hannah made some visits up the Cleveland coast to sell fish to the steelworkers' families. They had done this before, keeping back as much fish as they could carry from the dealer who waited above the staith with his donkey carts. It was a real tramp for them, carrying the fish baskets on their heads padded with wreaths, but they could make a bit of extra money that way, before the worst weather set in. They were getting the reputation of being sharp business women.

The flither pickers began to talk of a trek. This was something they often had to do during the winter months, but now they thought it best to get it done whilst it was still autumn, before the worst weather came.

There was such a great amount of flither picking and mussel picking done in our bay that the shellfish would become few, and small at that. So the women would organise a trek. They'd set off with a great load of sacks and swills and walk away down the coast in search of a right good supply. They had to go past Whitby, ignoring the limpets there, for they were needed by the Whitby pickers and a large supply they needed too. So our Sandwick women had to go to the scaur way past Whitby and a good fifteen miles that was. It was all a bit of a fuss and a palaver; they had to find relations or friends to stay overnight with in Whitby.

We'd send the donkey carts over the cliffs to carry the flithers back. Then the women would be up early the next morning and walking back to get the caving and skaning done, so's not to lose another day's fishing.

"Can't I come with you this time?" I begged Mam, when she and Hannah were making their plans.

"Nay," said Mam. "A trek's no outing and you'll stay to see to Billy and your grandpa . . . though I wish you might be back in school once your grandpa is himself again."

I sighed and opened my mouth to make more arguments, but I caught Aunt Hannah looking at me, so I shut my mouth and went out onto the staith.

I didn't want to be getting back to school at all, but I hated Grandpa being sick. Mam talked to Hannah about it and I could tell she was worried. The thing was that you couldn't really say what was wrong. He lay in bed all day and refused to eat most of the food that we carried up to him. Even Billy couldn't rouse him. Miriam said there was nothing to be done. She said that he was suffering from grief and that had to run its course. We should leave him be, she said, and he'd come back to us in his own good time. But the weeks went by and he kept to his bed.

I sat out there on the top staith, remembering how happy I'd been when I was a little girl. Grandma Esther would wrap me up warm in my bonnet and shawl and I'd go out with Grandpa in all but the worst of weather and we'd sit up there on the top staith. We never sat alone, for every person passing would stop to speak. Sometimes we'd be surrounded by a great gang of children, listening to Grandpa's stories. I was so proud to be sat up there on Grandpa's knee, so proud to be his grandchild. He'd tell stories of shipwrecks, of smuggling, of our lifeboats and the different coxswains, the rescues that he'd made himself, but my favourite story came from a time way back: the story of Simon Wise.

Grandpa would tell how a mysterious stranger had come from the forests over Pickering way and his name, so he said, was Simon Wise. He'd taken to fishing and had gone out one night with an old fisherman who'd befriended him. That night they'd been attacked by a French ship, a man-o'-war. Simon Wise had told his friend not to be afraid and he'd taken up his bow and arrow and shot every Frenchman that tried to board the small boat. The last few members of the crew surrendered and asked Simon Wise aboard. It turned out to be a pirate ship, loaded with stolen gold that the pirates offered to Simon Wise in payment for their lives, but he sent the pirates on their way, telling them not to pick on small fishing boats again, and gave away all the gold to the poor fisher-folk of the coast. He then returned to the forest he came from and later became known in other parts of the country as the outlaw Robin Hood.

Mam, Dad and Mrs Ruswarp were making plans for Irene's wedding. It was to be as soon as we could get it arranged, keeping a bit of decency, as Dad said, for the banns to be read up in Mulgrave Chapel. So we'd got the date fixed for late November and, although it was to be a rushed do, my dad insisted that we'd make it a fine wedding and hold our heads high. We'd have all the traditional fun and frills: a reception in the village hall and dancing late into the night, and of course we'd have John Ruswarp's coble hauled up on the beach to be decorated with flags and bunting and paper flowers. Mam said she wanted to get the trek done first, then we'd have an outing to Whitby to buy the stuff for Irene's wedding. Mary Jane and me were to be bridesmaids. Mam said two were enough in the circumstances, instead of the usual six.

I got up early on the morning of the trek and Billy and

me walked along the beach to set them on their way. When we reached Caedmon's Cliff, Mam sent us back.

"And you see you get Billy back safe," she said. "The tide's on the turn so don't dawdle."

I didn't argue as I once might have done. "Yes, Mam," I answered meek enough, and after we'd watched them trudge away beneath the cliffs I took his hand and I did take care, for after what Hannah had told me I could see why Mam had taken fright when I let Billy wander on the cliffs. I'd thought a bit more about our Billy, too. He was a fine little brother really and I wouldn't be without him. We played follow-my-leader as we went back to the village and I let him be the leader. I even enjoyed seeing him so delighted when he made me crawl on all fours over the scaur and walk backwards, twice round Plosher Rock.

It was quiet in the village for most of the women had gone on the trek, leaving only the young and the old, and the men still resting, having got back from the sea in the early hours. Billy and me sat on the top staith where Grandpa used to sit.

Old Walter Snaith came and sat with us for a while, working away at one of his baskets. Walter made all the baskets we needed for our work: swills for collecting flithers, skeps for the long lines and big fish-baskets, too. He asked after my grandpa and said that it was a sad thing indeed. He'd known Grandpa well; they'd been lads together.

Walter finished his basket and got up to go. He was to take the donkey carts over the cliffs to fetch the bait that was gathered. He said he must round up some of the lads to help him. I wished I could have gone too, but I was needed at home, so I sat tight.

Miriam came out into her front to get a bit of sun while she did her knitting. Miriam had no husband and no son, but every spare moment she was knitting away at a gansey. It was never for a particular person, just a medium-sized gansey for whoever needed it most. Miriam did all the things that any mother did, though she'd no children of her own. It was as though the whole village were her children. Old or young, she mothered us all; I can't think how we'd have managed without her.

She did well enough living by herself and though she wasn't rich, she didn't lack for anything either. Sometimes we paid her for her simples and her nursing care, but if folk were short they'd pay her with fish or by helping with repairs to her neat cottage on the front. However poor, none were turned away from her door.

I watched her knitting in the sun and wondered if I dare ask her about William and the dreadful thing that had happened. There was nobody else around and I could see that she wasn't busy for once. Still I was reluctant; you didn't call on Miriam unless something was up – sickness or childbirth or death. You didn't call to pass the time of day, but the strange thing was that Miriam looked up and beckoned me.

I went over to her gate.

"Well, Liza Welford, so you're left to mind your Billy."

She continued with her knitting while she spoke, bony fingers working fast, not needing to look at what she did . . . like all the women in our bay.

"Aye," I answered. "We've set them on their way."

I couldn't think when I'd looked close at Miriam before, she never stopped still long enough as a rule. Fine wrinkles creased her forehead and cheeks. Her hair worn thin and silver was tucked neatly beneath her blue cotton Sandwick bonnet. Light grey eyes peered sharp at me through small gold-rimmed spectacles.

"You'll be missing your Esther, I dare say?"

"Aye," I repeated it with a sigh.

"She were right fond of you," said Miriam, "and you'll miss her sore, but you must treasure what you remember and that way you'll still have her."

I nodded. She was right, but there was something more I needed to ask.

"That night," I said. "That night when Grandma Esther died, she tried to tell me something. It was about my mam. She tried to tell how Mam's young brother William Archer was drowned."

Miriam's head jerked up and the wrinkles in her forehead gathered tighter still, but she nodded me to have my say.

"Well . . . she never got it said, but I've asked Aunt Hannah and she's told me what a terrible thing it was and how it'd upset my mam, but she didn't know what happened when they went off looking. She said it was you who brought Mam back."

"So I did and there's no mystery as to where she was. She was here in my cottage till late that night, though as for what went on . . . that's between her and me."

Miriam folded her knitting and got up from her chair. I thought she was sending me off. I thought I'd pried where I shouldn't. I was ready to go but Miriam pointed to Billy, who'd been slinging pebbles against her wall.

"Fetch your Billy through to my garden, then you may take a drink of tea with me."

Chapter Seven

It was a special treat to go into Miriam's garden and Billy came willingly enough. It spread a long way up onto the hillside from the back of her cottage; the biggest garden in the village, packed with herbs and flowers. There was lavender to crush and sniff, and liquorice root to clean and chew. I led Billy through Miriam's kitchen that was hung with bunches of herbs drying for the winter use. I would have liked to go out with him, but there were more important things to worry about.

Miriam put on her kettle and made me sit. A proper visitor I was and I wasn't used to it. She brought our tea and sat beside her fire, thoughtful for a moment, then she spoke.

"I'll tell what I think I should, though I'll not tell all. No one will ever know it all but your mam and me."

I nodded, feeling the importance of what she said.

"It's a long way back now, but it's one of those days that stick in your memory. You'd like to forget it, but you can't. I was here, busy with something – I can't think what. I knew there'd been a commotion on the beach. I didn't go out, I knew I'd hear soon enough if I was needed. I looked out once, I recall, and saw Martha down there by herself, but I thought nowt of that. Then I glanced out a while later and there she was in exactly the same spot. She'd never moved. The second time I looked something bothered me, something about the stillness of her, and I decided to go down.

"I passed someone on the way and I heard that William was lost and that they were all searching for him. When I

got closer to Martha, I really took fright. I could see that she'd not moved, not one speck, and the sea was up to her knees . . . her face blank, like a person dead. I ran and took hold of her, but she was stiff and cold, staring out to sea, and her just a young girl like you."

When Miriam told me that I bit my lips hard to keep back the tears. I knew I was being told something very secret. I must treat it with respect.

"I could tell what had happened," said Miriam. "I knew when I saw her face that William had drowned and that what she wanted was to rush into the sea and follow him, but fear stopped her. So there she stood, letting the sea come up. She couldn't go to meet it, but she couldn't resign herself to living either. Aye," said Miriam, tapping me on the arm, "you let the tears fall, for it was a thing no young girl should have to face."

I did as she said; I let the tears fall and wept for my mam and her brother. When I'd dried my eyes and calmed myself, Miriam finished her telling.

"I got her to move, though it was difficult, but I got her back up here and she stayed with me for the rest of the day. Outside they were searching for William, but I knew it was in vain. William was beyond help, it was Martha who needed me. We talked and talked and I'll not say all, but a struggle took place and by the time night came, Martha had somehow gotten the strength to go on with her life. It was with grim determination though and she was never a child again, not after that.

"Now Liza," she said, putting her hands on my shoulders to make me really take notice, "I've said what I thought right and what Esther in her wisdom wanted you to know, but the time will come when you must speak to your mam. That would be for the best."

It left me quiet and sad, almost wishing I'd never asked. I thanked her and called our Billy in from the garden.

I thought about my talk with Miriam all night and

who's a fine lady now?" He laughed and smiled as he hadn't done since Grandma Esther died.

No matter how I tried I couldn't concentrate on the shelling and Mam let me off. She let me run down to the Ruswarps' with the news, for I was bursting to tell and she said she'd get on better without me.

Mary Jane threw herself on the floor, laughing and laughing, till Mrs Ruswarp got worried. It was only when I showed the letter that she calmed down and they both believed me.

We talked of nothing else that week and made such preparations for our outing. Mam with her canny ways insisted that we should make it our shopping day for the wedding and save ourselves the expense of another trip. As the transport was to be provided we could all go – Mam, Dad, Irene, Mrs Ruswarp, Mary Jane and me. We'd been worried about Grandpa, but as usual Miriam came to our rescue. She said she'd look after Billy and take Grandpa his meals. We were excited and it was only the thought of Grandpa's unhappiness that marred our pleasure.

We'd tried so hard to cheer him and get him to take interest again, but nothing roused him. Not Irene's wedding, not our prize picture, not the coming bairn.

I kept my book in our loft in a fine woven basket that Grandma Esther had made for me one Eastertide. I'd never had a book. There were books at school, but they were worn and had to be shared and only for use in school time. Then we had our family bible, our family record of births and deaths, which Dad kept in a special chest. This bea.. bound book was quite different, a special book of my own. No one in the bay had such a thing. I don't think I'd ever have tried to read it if it wasn't that the picture man had written a special message inside it.

The first night that I had it, I carried my candle up to

bed and looked again at my new treasure. I opened the cover and saw the picture man's writing. I thought, fancy doing that. Fancy writing in a brand new book, on such a fresh white page. It said: *For Liza, hoping that within these pages she will discover that learning can be for her.* I was puzzled, I didn't know what it meant. I remembered how I'd told him 'learning had nowt to do with me', then worried that I'd been rude. Still, rudeness or not, it had brought me this book. He means me to read it, I thought. I'd have to be very careful if I were to read it. I wouldn't have to dirty these crisp pages or mark the cover. I'd have to scrub my hands real well if I were to read it.

I turned the pages delicately, past the Contents and on to the story. I glanced at each page as I passed, then stopped. I stared at the title of Chapter Two: *A North Yorkshire Fisher Maiden.* Fisher maidens, I thought. Why, who'd put them in a book? I looked down the page and began to read.

A group of tall, handsome fisher-girls who were down by the edge of the tide – such girls as you would hardly see anywhere else in England for strength and straightness, for roundness of form and bright, fresh healthfulness of countenance.

Why, I thought, it's about girls like us . . . like me or Irene or Mary Jane.

I read on and found more to interest me. It was about a fisher-girl called Barbara Burdas, who'd two young men both loving her, one of them a fisherman named David Andoe and the other was Hartas Theyn, a rather shabby squire's son.

I turned back to the beginning and started to read it properly. I'd never read anything like it before. It was a love story but very sad, with things going wrong. Dreadful things happened to Barbara Burdas, but then such things happened in our own bay, I knew that well enough. I read and read until my candle guttered and Irene came grumbling up to bed, fishing around in the dark.

Chapter Eight

We'd all dressed smart on the Saturday morning, scrubbed clean and wearing our Sunday best. Mam and Irene in their silk bonnets and me and Mary Jane laced tight in our best boots. The pony and trap arrived on time and we climbed in chatting and smiling at the treat of it all.

John Ruswarp came to set us off on our way. He'd have liked to be coming but wasn't allowed, for he mustn't see the stuffs for our wedding clothes – bad luck that would be. John ran beside us as the trap set off. He ran till he could keep up no more, with Irene waving and blushing till he was out of sight.

We enjoyed the drive into Whitby, passing through villages we knew well, holding our heads high, giggling as folk turned to watch, wondering what was up.

Whitby was always busy on a Saturday, what with the street traders and the market and the ladies and gentlemen buying their goods. We went straight to the photographic studios, for we couldn't wait to see our picture. The studio had a double shop front, new and grand, with flowers and plants arranged in the windows and flower designs on the glass, with dark velvet curtains behind.

We went in and stood shy and uncomfortable in the waiting room, staring at the leather upholstery and rich drapes. A lady sat there with her child and its nurse, all dressed very fine. The lady wore a cream dress with lace and tucks and a row of bows to show off her tiny waist. The nurse was dressed in black and white, but the best silk. I felt sorry for the baby; its fat cheeks bulged and it fretted and peered from beneath a bonnet that was so bedecked with lace and frills that the poor bairn could hardly see.

I tried not to stare, but that was hard for I wanted to remember it all. The lady fetched out a tiny lace handkerchief when we came in. She held it to her nose, turning her head to whisper to the nurse as if she thought us most inferior – and us all scrubbed and in our finery.

I was glad when the picture man came through to us and greeted us real pleased and polite, ignoring the lady with her miserable child. He invited us upstairs to another room and there on the wall in a carved wooden frame hung the picture of me and Mary Jane. At the sight of it we lost all shyness and talked and laughed. The picture was so full of life, you'd think we could've jumped up at any moment and splashed away into the sea.

The picture man said that he was very proud that we'd won him a prize in such an important competition. He brought out two smaller prints of our picture that he'd set in neat frames and he gave them to us to hang on the wall at home.

Mam said as how it was so kind of the picture man to have sent me such a lovely book.

"But did you read it, young lady?" he asked.

Well, once he'd got me going on that, I talked on and on, telling how I'd read it once and then read it again. How I'd told the story to Mary Jane and then how Mam and Irene had let me sit up late each night, reading the story out loud to them and how we'd all thought the story wonderful and sad and how we felt flat now that we were getting near to the end, and thinking we'd have to start at the beginning again.

"I thought it might be just the thing," he said. "Do you know of Mary Linskill, the lady who wrote the story? A Whitby lady she was, though sadly she died a few years back."

"Whitby?" I said. "Did she really live in Whitby? Did you

know her?" The picture man smiled at my surprise. "I did indeed," he said.

Mam and Dad and the others stood quiet and smiling, letting me chatter on and on about my wonderful book. The picture man was pleased, I could tell, pleased that he'd found something that had given such pleasure and interest.

"I have to make a photograph of a baby now," he said, "but when I've done, I could show you where Mary lived and tell you more about her."

I was delighted at that, but Mam said though it was most kind, he shouldn't waste his valuable time.

No, he insisted, he'd enjoy doing that, so we arranged to meet him in the market place at noon.

Mam explained that we'd shopping to do for Irene's wedding. The picture man congratulated Irene, making her blush, then he said he'd like to make a studio portrait of her, for she'd a very fine face. That made her blush even more.

We swept through the waiting room, our noses in the air.

"They'll see our picture when they go through," Mary Jane whispered.

Our bridesmaids' shopping was soon done. We'd got fine white silk for our dresses, with lace to stitch at the necks; a yard of blue velvet ribbon each for our sashes and new white stockings to go with our white boots.

"We'll be fine as any lady," said Mary Jane.

Irene couldn't make up her mind about the stuff for her dress, so we left her with Mam and Mrs Ruswarp and went with Dad to the market place. We loved going to look at the stalls and Dad let us sit up at the counter of Jacksons, beneath the cheerful striped awnings. We both had a dainty glass dishful of hokey-pokey ice cream, a rare treat that froze our tongues and made our teeth ache as we crunched the tiny slivers of ice.

Dad was in a fine mood, calling out to his Whitby friends that he hadn't seen for a time, passing on the latest gossip, telling everyone about our prize-winning photograph and worrying over the news from South Africa. There were rumours of sickness and fever, and our lads suffering from poor rations. Many folk were saying that they ought to be brought back home.

When we all met up again, Irene had found the material she liked, and ribbons and lace to make it bonny. The picture man found us by the fish stall that belonged to Hannah Smith, who we all called Trickey. Mrs Smith had a reputation of being able to sell fish to anyone, so crafty and clever she was.

"You shouldn't stand talking too long to Mrs Smith," said the picture man, "she'll talk you into buying a haddock to take back to Sandwick Bay."

We followed the picture man up to Church Street, then off to the right through one of the dark alleys that open into a yard, Blackburn's Yard, just as small and cramped as our own.

"She never lived here?" I said. "Not that lady who wrote the story?"

"Yes," said the picture man. He pointed out a small cottage. "This is where she was born and this," he said, pointing to a rather newer cottage, "this is where the family moved to later."

"But was she not rich and clever?" I asked.

"She was clever enough, but she was never rich."

"Is that so?" said Mam. "She wrote that lovely book, but never had money?"

"Her father was one of the constables," said the picture man. "A respectable working man. Sometimes, when he took female prisoners, he would keep them in the cottage with his family. Mary had the job of carrying the food to them. I think she often heard their sad stories. A strange start in life, I should think."

Mam nodded her head. "Strange indeed."

"But how did she get to write her stories?" I asked.

"Ah well, young lady, she went to school. Her mam was keen for her to do that, so she went to school and she worked real hard."

"Where did she go to school?" I asked.

"Here, in Whitby, a school like yours no doubt, though I don't believe she had anyone as kind as Miss Hindmarch for her teacher."

"But when did she write her stories?"

"Ah, that was later. She worked as a milliner at first . . . then she became a governess and spent many years away from Whitby. It was in her middle years that she returned to Whitby and set about earning her living from writing her stories. After her father died she tried to keep her mother and sister with what she earned. Those were very hard times for Mary."

"Did she not earn money from her books?"

"Not at first. Often she became so short of money that there was little food in the house. Mary would dread her friends visiting, for she had nothing to offer them. Sometimes she could not walk out for she'd no boots to wear."

That shocked me, for no visitor at our cottage would ever go short of food and though a fisher-girl like me might go barefoot on the sand, no decent person could walk through town without boots.

"Her friends lost patience with her at times," he said, though he smiled as he remembered it. "They thought she was mad to be trying to write, when she could have earned a respectable living as a governess. That would have been more seemly, more ladylike."

The picture man laughed and I could tell that he admired Mary's stubbornness. "Mary was determined," he said, "and she succeeded in the end."

"So she did get to be rich?" said Mam.

"She never really did. She managed to buy a house up in Springvale, on the smart side, and she lived there with her mother, but it was not long before she died. It is only now that her books are selling well. It seems sad that Mary never lived to enjoy it."

We all stood quiet, struck by the shame of it all.

"But now, young lady," said the picture man, "I have another gift that I hope you will all enjoy."

From his pocket he took another book, just as beautifully bound as the first. My mouth dropped open and my hands went out.

"Well," said Irene. "Two books, two books. I've never heard the like."

"*The Haven Under The Hill*," I read from the stamped gold title letters. "It's by Mary, too. Oh I can't wait to start to read."

Mam and Dad were overwhelmed and they couldn't thank him enough. I forgot my manners and opened the book, pointing out words to Mary Jane. "Why, it's about Whitby, this is. It tells about Hild and Caedmon and the old street Haggerlythe."

I'd been so excited, the time had flown by and we'd had to find the pony and trap and set off back to Sandwick Bay.

We were tired after our busy day, though we were laughing and chattering and I clutched tight to my precious book. A chill wind came off the sea and the sinking sun painted patterns over the hills and valleys. When we reached the top of our steep bank, we fell silent. There was John Ruswarp waiting for us by the stile, where the heather begins. There was another young man with him, a man I didn't recognise, tall and thin and sunburnt, dressed in Army clothes.

We stared, but Mam climbed down from the trap. She stretched up her hands to the strange young man, touching his cheek.

"Our Frank," she said.

Chapter Nine

I couldn't believe it was our Frank. I don't know how Mam recognised him straight off like that. It was more than eighteen months since he'd gone off to the fighting, but I would never have thought a lad could change so much in that time.

He'd always been strong and healthy, had our Frank, with his blue eyes and ruddy cheeks. Well built he'd been, with good muscles. It had been no effort to him to heave a coble up onto the sands, or swing a little lass up into the air. This man was pitifully thin, his cheeks sallow beneath the sunburn and his thick golden hair bleached white and sparse.

John came to help Irene down from the trap. I think he'd been shocked when Frank turned up knocking at the Ruswarps' door, after he'd got no reply from our cottage. Irene went up to Frank and hugged him, the tears pouring down her face.

"Our Frank . . . our Frank," she said.

It was Dad who voiced what was on all our minds. He followed Irene down and took Frank by the hand when Mam moved back, then he clapped his arm round Frank's shoulder, hugging the thin trembling body to his chest.

"Eeeh lad . . . what ails? Are you hurt?"

Frank clung to my dad for a moment as though he were a bairn, but then he pulled back, showing us he'd still got some pride.

"I've been sick, that's all. I've had the fever like a lot of them, but I'm better now. Nay," he said, coming over to me, "this grand lady is never our Liza? Have you not a kiss for your brother?"

I had felt shy, him looking so different and all, but it was his own cheeky way of talking and I threw my arms around him, though I didn't like the bony feel of his shoulders beneath the army jacket.

"I cannot swing you up onto my shoulder, such a fine grown lady you are," he said, and though they laughed, Mam's lips tightened and I knew she thought that he'd not have the strength to do it either.

We let the pony and trap go back to Whitby and we all walked down the steep hill to Sandwick, carrying our parcels. We'd much to tell Frank, both happy and sad, and we talked till late at night.

Frank only had a few days' leave, then he had to get back to Scarborough where he was billeted. He'd not been able to come back in August with the others as he'd been so ill. He made light of his sickness but the weakness and fits of trembling that came over him told us that he'd been very ill indeed. There was a great deal of talking done, but most of it was on our side. Try as he might, Dad could not get Frank to tell what he'd been doing, away at the war. Once Mam tried to get him to say, but all he'd answer was that he was shamed to speak of it, and begged her not to ask.

Frank spent much of his time sitting beside Grandpa's bed. I don't think they did much talking, but they seemed to have a quiet understanding. Billy ran to hide whenever Frank looked his way.

The night before Frank was due to return, Irene came up late to bed. She'd been sitting out on the top staith with Frank and John, all talking softly together, though Mam kept saying that they'd all be getting chilled. Irene lay beside me quietly sobbing; I could feel the heaving of her shoulders and hear the catch of her breath.

"What is it?" I asked.

"'Tis nowt," she said. "Nowt, but Frank has talked John into giving up his plans for the Army."

60

"What? Are you not glad of that? You didn't want him going off?"

"Oh I'm glad all right. I'm that relieved I can't say how much, but it's what Frank said that's shaken me. It's bad out there, where the fighting is, much worse than I thought. Frank says he's shamed to speak of it to Mam and Dad, but he managed to tell John, for he couldn't bear to let John follow him."

"Well," I said. "All that fighting and killing must be dreadful, but why is he so shamed? Soldiers are supposed to fight, aren't they?"

"Aye, but Frank says it's the women and children involved in it all that he cannot feel right about. He says they've found many a farmhouse with the men away fighting and they've turned out the mother and her bairns and they've had orders to burn the place to the ground. They've burnt everything – their food, their clothes – and left them with nowt but what they stand in."

"Nay," I said, "but what happens to them?"

"He says they're herded away into camps, where they live in tents, cramped together, sleeping on the ground. They've nowt to drink but fever-ridden water. They cannot keep themselves clean and they've very little food. They're dying in those camps, he says, mothers and bairns, dying like flies."

I was silent then, I knew why he was shamed. I couldn't see how a decent lad like our Frank could be part of all that, then I realised that since he'd volunteered himself he'd no choice but to do it or be killed.

We all went up to the top of the bank to set Frank on his way, but we were quiet. His homecoming hadn't been the happy one we'd wanted. Mam clung to him when it was time to go and Dad told him that his lines would still be waiting, and then we had to let him be on his way.

I sat on Plosher Rock, staring out to sea, watching the wake of the boats till they vanished. Nearby, the waves burst white and fizzing, lapping at the driftwood beyond my feet. Far out, the swell was dark blue, patterned like mackerel skin with the lighter blue of the sky. All heaving gently in a quiet breathing rhythm . . . just a light stirring here and there, a hint of the power beneath.

The low sun warmed my back and apart from the guilt of knowing there was work to be done and the unspoken chiding that'd come from Mam, I was happy. Content to sit for the moment.

The weeks had passed and we were well into November, though the weather had stayed fine for that time of year. Irene's dress was ready and beautiful, hanging from the beam in our loft. My dress just needed the lace and frill, and we'd been to chapel to hear the banns being read. Mam and Mrs Ruswarp had been sitting up late into the night, getting all the stitching done, while I read to them from *The Haven Under The Hill*. We all enjoyed the story just as much as the first one and I often thought about the Whitby woman who'd written it. Irene was happy and looking forward; she was even looking forward to her baby being born, though I couldn't be understanding that. Still, I loved the thought of being an auntie . . . I had such plans: I'd make little presents, I'd carve a boat out of wood, the way I'd seen Grandpa do it.

I sat there thinking about it all, but then noticed the sky changing. Grey clouds heavy with rain came over from the horizon, heading inland, though the sun still shone through, sharp and red, in spiky rays. The clouds came over very sudden and it went dark and cold. I saw red flecks of the sun's reflection in the nearest waves. I shuddered. Flecked with blood, I thought. Great spots of rain began to fall as I ran home thinking of my dad out there on the sea.

It was late that night that the storm really broke. I

couldn't remember another storm like it. Mam had sent me and Irene up to bed but we couldn't sleep, what with worrying about Dad and John who were both out in it all. We heard footsteps passing to and fro beneath our window and a lot of shouting going on. At last we heard our own door slam hard, caught in the wind . . . we knew Mam had gone out.

"I'll not lie abed in this," said Irene and she was up and pulling on her frock that was so tight now and wrapping her shawl criss-cross, to fasten at the back. I couldn't stop her so I helped her, then dressed myself as well. I followed her down the ladder, past Billy rolling around in Mam's bed. He jumped out when he saw us and pattered downstairs behind us, his thin legs bare beneath his white shirt.

"Get back, get back," we told him, but he followed and we couldn't make him stay.

The blast was so strong, we couldn't get the door open at first, then when we did, it slammed back so sharp our Billy screamed. He wasn't caught by it, just scared, and I got hold of him, suddenly scared myself. Mam came running up and pushed us back inside. She was soaked and her hair all snarzly. I thought she'd shout at us for coming out, but the tense, low voice she spoke with frightened me more.

"We'll have to get the boat out," she said. "We must help fetch the men. Irene, you run to the Pickerings'. Liza, keep Billy here . . . keep him safe for me."

Then she was gone and Irene after her with the door banging and banging till I caught it on the sneck. Billy was white and shivering so I took him back upstairs and crept into Mam's bed beside him. I cuddled up and he fell asleep. I couldn't sleep though and I wondered about Grandpa – surely he couldn't be sleeping through all this commotion. I got up and made some tea and carried a cup into him. He lay on his back, staring wide-eyed at the ceiling. I put the cup beside him.

"There's a terrible storm, Grandpa. They're wanting to get the boat out."

He never moved or spoke and I went back to Billy. I sat full-dressed on the edge of Mam's bed. I hated sitting there, I wanted to be out and seeing what was going on. Then Irene came back, puffing and blowing, stamping frantic up our stairs, straight into Grandpa's room.

"You must come," she cried. "You must come. We've no men, they're all out there, beyond the bay, and they cannot bring the boats in."

I followed her into his room. She ran round his bed, pulling at the blankets, her hair streaming water, sprinkling wet over the sheets.

"They'll be lost if you don't come," but Grandpa stared blank at her.

Then Mam came flying up the stairs as drenched as Irene.

"I cannot move him," Irene's voice rose. "I cannot make him come."

Mam stood at the foot of his bed and spoke again in that strained, quiet voice.

"We cannot launch the boat without you be coxswain. Get out of your bed, Isaac Welford, and think what your Esther would have said."

I'd never heard Mam speak so sharp to him before and I caught my breath at it, but Grandpa looked at Mam and I could tell he'd understood and listened to what she'd said.

"Who is there to crew?"

"There's Walter Snaith and his grandson, there's John Pickering and old Tom Danby and a gang of lads all willing to row, but there's none as knows the sandbanks and the rocks, there's none as can guide her out but you."

Still Grandpa shook his head. "Nay. They're only old

fellas and young lads and it'll take every one of them. There's none left to launch her."

"We can launch her," said Irene. "Us women can do the launching."

Grandpa shook his head again. "Women? It takes strong men to launch that boat. Aye, and plenty of 'em."

"Hannah knows what to do. She's helped before."

"Nay, we've never had women in those racks. Ye'd not stand a chance."

Irene covered her face with her hands, near despairing.

Mam spoke firm again. "Now listen you here, Isaac Welford. If you can be coxswain and those lads can man her, then we can launch her."

At last Grandpa seemed to gather himself together. A spark of his old self gleamed in his face and he laughed out loud.

"All right, my lass, all right. If you lot can launch her, then we will man her. Now get me out of this bed."

He held up his arms and Mam and Irene grabbed hold and pulled him out. Mam picked up his gansey from the dresser and eased it over his nightshirt.

"Fetch Dan's spare, Liza, and his oilskins, too."

I ran back to Mam's room and fetched my dad's gear and watched as they got Grandpa dressed. He was shaky and stiff-legged – he'd not been out of his bed for weeks – but he bellowed questions at Mam and she answered fast and clear. Then off they went, Grandpa stumping down our stairs, and I turned back to Billy.

He was awake and out of bed and I wasn't going to stay at home, not now. I got Billy's coat and wrapped him up good and warm, pushing on his boots. "You stay by me," I said. "You stay by me whatever happens."

Billy nodded, his eyes wide and round.

Chapter Ten

The wind was so strong that it was hard to breathe at first and I nearly turned round and went back inside. Such a rush there was, folk shouting and surging like a great wave down to the boathouse. I grabbed our Billy tight and we became part of the wave, down the staith and onto the beach we went.

They'd already got the lights out, big cans with a paraffin light that we call ducks. They'd carried them down the lifeboat ramp where they lit up the beach.

The sun was just beginning to show and a dim grey light lit the sea. The sea as I'd never seen it before. Our bay was filled with white foam, seething like a boiling cauldron, the white only broken by grey breakers that turned black as they burst, sending creamy spray flying high into the sky. I turned my head sharp, catching rainbow flashes from the corners of my eyes, and far out were glimpses of dark shapes that vanished, then reappeared: our small fishing fleet, so tossed that you couldn't see them clear.

Billy pulled my hand, pointing and shouting with delight. I turned to see them pulling open the doors of the lifeboat house and the great shining prow of our lifeboat gleaming in the light of the ducks. Our lifeboat that we loved, even worshipped – the spirit of our village, as near a holy thing as we could have.

The boat was full of young lads and the boathouse full of women. Mam helped Grandpa up the ladder and she and Hannah half-lifted, half-threw him into the stern. Some of the lads who'd come to row were swamped in their dads' oilskins, but the scratch crew were all in place. Grandpa gave the signal to Walter Snaith who fired the warning pistol. Mam and Hannah and the other women gathered round the winch, as many as could find a place to hold, and Irene let loose the safety chain. Slowly, bit by bit and jerking to the side, the boat was lowered onto its carriage, then steered out onto the ramp.

"Away . . . let her away," shouted Grandpa and our great boat rumbled down the slipway, coming to rest steady on its carriage on the sand.

Then came the launchers' hardest part. The women formed up in the launching racks, two by two, ready to push her out to the sea. Hannah stood at the front shouting instructions and I saw that Mary Jane had gone to pull on the ropes with other girls and lads.

"Right," I said to Billy. "We're needed."

I ran, pulling Billy with me, and grabbed the rope beside Mary Jane.

"You get that rope and you pull hard," I yelled at him.

I saw Mam in one of the racks, straining with the weight, then Irene slotted herself in behind. I could see that bothered Mam, she was worrying about Irene and her bairn, but strong arms pulled Irene from the rack and a great powerful body took her place. It was Nelly Wright and I could have hugged her. Irene didn't stay to argue, but went to push at the back.

The women strained, but the boat didn't move.

"I'll call," shouted Hannah. "One, two and away. One, two and away."

I think every person in our bay was there, everyone who could stand. I saw Mary Jane's granny and Old Miriam hauling on the ropes, and Annie Lythe, who'd no family to save, was there with her oldest lad, pulling and heaving with the rest. At last the carriage shifted a bit and a cheer went up from the lads above. Once it started it moved slow but steady across the sand till we neared the water's edge.

We dropped our ropes then and ran to push at the back. I lost Billy at that moment, but I didn't stop to think, just ran and pushed with the others, pushed for all I was worth. The women in the racks trudged out into the waves.

I hardly noticed when we first reached the sea. My skirts were so drenched and cold that the water made no difference, but when we got further out I knew all right, for a wicked underswell pulled at me, trying to pluck my feet from under my legs. It caught me and I fell; the freezing salt waves punched me in the face. I was left wallowing as the others went on. Such a rage of anger rose in me that I dragged myself upright, shouting and screaming abuse – abuse at the sea, shaking my fists, tears bursting from my eyes.

Then I stopped. Pushing ahead was Mam, past her waist in the swirling mass. My mam, who was so feared of the sea that she couldn't cross a causeway, couldn't bear to wet her toes. I didn't know how she was doing it, wading out like that. And what of Irene, following on behind, with that little baby growing inside her, the one I'd be an auntie for. I remembered Billy; that was my job. If Billy got lost or hurt it'd be my fault. I turned back to look for him.

Billy was hiding beside the lifeboat ramp and he'd found his friend Jackie Lythe. I suppose they thought they'd got a bit of shelter from the wind, but they were both shivering down there.

"Get 'em up and make 'em run." It was Miriam, who stood beside me pointing her bony finger at the two lads. "Get 'em out. They can run with the ropes now. They're coming away from the racks and we'll all be needed again."

So I made Billy and Jackie go back down the beach. Mam and Irene and the others were coming towards us through the waves. Two of the lads climbed over the sides of the boat and untied the launching ropes, flinging them down to Hannah below.

We all had to get ready now for the last big haul. The ropes had to be dragged along the beach either way and tugged real sharp, to catapult the lifeboat from its carriage, forward into the sea. We all waited on Grandpa's signal, for he had to choose just the right moment – when a wave had gone, but before the next one came.

"Away now . . . away," came the cry. We took hold and pulled and shouted, till we were running fast.

"Away now. Away!" we yelled, as though the strength of our voices would add to the weight on the ropes. Billy hauled away, just in front of me. He was running so fast I swear his feet never touched the ground, but swung to and fro. I didn't see that I was running into a rock and I fell hard, rolling quick to the side, for I knew I'd be trampled if I didn't shift.

I rolled on the sand as the cry changed.

"She's off." The rope fell slack and the boat plunged forward into the waves, the oars pulling back, not quite together but strong enough to move her, dipping sharp, up and down.

It was Billy who found me then. I heard his voice. "Liza, Liza," and I shouted back to him.

"I thought you'd got squashed," he said.

"I'm worse than squashed," I said. "Pull me up. We must find our mam."

I wasn't the only one who'd fallen; there were women helping each other up and rubbing knees and shins, all along the beach. We gathered together by the ducks. They gave little heat, but they seemed to give a bit of comfort. Hannah said that the bairns and the old ones should all go home, as there was no more we could do, but none would go. We huddled together, watching the heavy boat that looked so fragile now, swinging up and down and out of sight. Giving us a glimpse, then nowt.

Mam rubbed Irene's hands. "Get yourself back," she said. "Get yourself back and into your bed."

"I'll not . . . not till they're fetched."

"They're doing grand," said Mam. "Who'd have thought those lads could row like that? They look to have reached the bank and be getting through."

We all looked, narrowing our eyes. The bank was the dangerous shallows at the mouth of our bay.

"There's none but Isaac Welford could have taken them through," said Hannah.

We waited helpless and dreary, but still no one would go home. Now we'd done our work and the effort was over, the freezing cold and wet made itself felt. The children began their shivering.

"Jump up and down," said Miriam. "Ye'll catch your deaths if ye stand there gawping. You show them, Liza, and you, Mary Jane. Jump about and clap your hands."

We tried, but we were too cold to get going properly.

"Ye must," said Miriam. "Ye'll freeze solid else. Ye'll turn into breakwaters, everyone of you, stuck for ever ont' beach."

So we laughed and tried again. Mary Jane started chanting a skipping rhyme:

> "*Souther wind souther,*
> *Bring father home to mother.*"

"That's it, lass," Miriam said. "They all know that," and she joined in, jumping up and down, her sodden skirts flapping round her skinny legs:

> "*Souther wind souther,*
> *Bring father home to mother.*"

Soon we were all at it, jumping to the rhythm, clapping hands, shouting as loud as we could. We went on to another rhyme:

> *"Northern sea, silver sea,*
> *Bring my daddy back to me,*
> *Hush the waves and still the sea,*
> *And bring my daddy back to me."*

All the mams joined in, bellowing it out faster and faster, and it warmed us and cheered us, till the cry went up.

"They're coming back!"

We stopped our jumping and ran to the water's edge, but we could see nothing clear. We waited in silence then, watching and screwing up our eyes. I thought I saw a moving shape, then it vanished, then I saw it again.

At last we could see that a small boat, tossing fiercely, was heading steadily for the shore. Then we saw another behind it.

"The cobles!" shouted Hannah, and a great cheer went up.

We couldn't see the lifeboat, but the small boats, taking courage from the lifeboat's presence, were coming in one by one. When the lifeboat did at last come into view there was more cheering and clapping of hands, but Mam and me stood next to Hannah.

"What is it?" said Mam. She knew Hannah of old.

Hannah shook her head. "There's not all there should be."

As the cobles came in we spread out along the beach to help drag them up. I kept looking for Dad, but I couldn't see him. When the lifeboat neared the shore we saw that it pulled a coble fastened by a line, and another upturned hull dragged behind that. I pulled at Mam's arm.

"Look," I said. "It's Dad's boat tied up behind. It's the *Sneaton Lass*."

Mam didn't move. The women gathered together to help get the boat out of the water. Irene came with Mrs Ruswarp and Mary Jane following.

"We cannot see the *Lily Belle*," Irene said. Then she followed Mam's gaze to the upturned hull dragged behind our *Sneaton Lass*.

"No," she whispered. "No."

Mam seemed to shake herself and put her arms round Irene. "You'll see. He'll be in the lifeboat, him and your dad. There's a line fastened. We'll find them in the boat."

We went down to help carry the ropes up to the winch. The men and lads were jumping over the sides into the shallows and the ones who'd fetched their cobles in came to help. The lifeboat was hauled back out of the water a deal more easy than she'd gone in.

We saw Dad inside the boat, but we couldn't see John. Uncle Frank was there and Sam Ruswarp; that made me think that John must be there too. Dad jumped over the edge and splashed towards us, but as he came near we saw that his face was grim and he slowed as though he didn't wish to reach us. He looked at Irene and Mrs Ruswarp, shaking his head.

"I'm sorry, lass," he said.

Sam Ruswarp came up behind them, hanging back from his mam as though shamed. But Mrs Ruswarp threw her arms round him and Mary Jane clung to them both.

Irene stared at Dad.

"Nay, nay . . . I've seen him. Look, he's there," she said, pointing to the lifeboat. "He's there in the boat. I saw his gansey. I know it well. I knitted it myself, the waves and herring-bone . . . I'd know it anywhere." She made to run towards the boat, but Dad caught her. He made her turn away from the sea, pushing her up the beach.

"He's gone lass, he's gone."

I stood there, cold and wet forgotten, watching them go, Mrs Ruswarp and Mary Jane following slowly with their Sam.

A choking sound behind me made me turn. There was

Mam bent double vomiting and Billy clutching frightened to her skirt. I ran to her and was shocked to feel the violent trembling that cut through her body. I couldn't think what else to do but hold her tight and press my hand against her forehead, as she'd done for me when I was sick as a bairn.

The retching stopped, but she still shook. Billy stared white-faced. He'd never seen his strong, quiet mam like this before and nor had I. It made me realise then that it had been no easy thing for her to go ploughing out into the sea, and of all people I should have known it.

"Come now Mam," I said. "We must get us home."

She nodded and let me lead her back, as though she were a child and I the mam. Billy followed, still holding tight to her skirt.

Just outside our cottage she stopped.

"I'm fine now Liza. I'm myself again. I must look to Irene and we must be thankful that our dad is spared."

"Yes Mam," I said, taking my arm away and letting her and Billy go in first. She was back to being in charge of us all again.

Chapter Eleven

Dad stayed at home the next night, even though the storm had eased. Our cottage was hushed. Even Billy was quiet, sitting on Dad's knee, watching for Mam's anxious face as she toiled up and down stairs carrying boiling water for Miriam's simples. Our Irene had a fever. Dad sat by the fire all the next day, staring into the grate. He should have been tired, but he couldn't sleep. Grandpa came down to sit with him and they talked in soft voices, saying the same things over and over again.

"I thought I had him," Dad would say. "I threw him a line and he fastened it. I thought they were safe, but then over they went, with a sudden cutting wave . . . right sudden, and over went the *Lily Belle*. I hauled young Sam out, no trouble, but I couldn't get hold of John. He was so close, just an arm's length, no more. Just an arm's length and I could have had him."

"Aye," said Grandpa. "It's always the same. You blame yourself when you shouldn't. I've seen more men go down than I can bear to think of and always you say, 'if I'd done this, if I'd done that'. You should not blame yourself. The sea takes those it wants."

"Aye, it does. But it grieves me so that it should take him. Like a son he was. I taught him all I know and now he's gone, leaving my poor lass like that."

Grandpa spoke very gentle. "He carried the stones you know . . . so Sam says. Pockets full of dogger, he says. They'd have pulled him straight down. You'd not have got him out . . . weighted like that."

It made me shudder when I heard that, but I shouldn't

have been surprised. There's plenty of the fishermen carry the stones, though it wasn't talked about much. They live in fear of a long struggling death if they're thrown overboard, so they don't learn to swim – don't learn on purpose – and they carry heavy stones in their pockets so as to make sure they'll sink straight down. Sam Ruswarp is one of the few who can swim, but I never knew about John.

I hated to think of John with his pockets full of dogger. He must have gone off up the coast deliberate like, looking for the heavy, egg-shaped ironstones that we call dogger, for they're only found where the Cleveland iron seam meets the sea.

Dad shook his head. "He never let on to me. All those times he went out with me and he never let on that he carried the stones. He must have been more feared than I knew."

They'd sit in silence then, Dad stroking Billy's hair, holding him close as though he daren't be letting him go. Then after a while it would all start again. Dad blaming himself and going over all that had happened and Grandpa saying what he could to comfort him.

They'd put Irene in Mam's bed and Miriam was nursing her. I wanted to go up to see her, but Mam said not.

"Soon," she said. "You can see her soon, but leave her to Miriam just now. We must get her to rest real well or . . ."

"What?" I said. "Or what? What more can happen now?"

Mam bit her lip. "I fear she could lose the bairn. She should not have been out last night, soaked and freezing and pushing at that heavy boat. I couldn't seem to stop her."

"There's nowt could have stopped her, Mam," I said.

I sat at our table lonely and useless. I wanted to do something. I wanted to be with Mary Jane, to whisper with her as we did when things went wrong, but this time I couldn't do that for Mary Jane's brother was drowned and it must be worse for her than me. So I sat on, miserable and sad.

It was late in the afternoon when there came a knock at the door. I opened it to find Mary Jane there with her mother. Mary Jane looked scared.

"It's Mam," she said. "She will not settle, but she must see Irene. I didn't know what to do for the best," and she burst into tears.

I pulled them both inside and Mam came to see what the noise was. Mrs Ruswarp came into the kitchen, calm but determined. "I want to see the lass, that's all. I need to see the lass."

Mam hesitated for a moment, then nodded her head. "Of course you must." She led the way upstairs.

I took Mary Jane to sit with me. I put my arms round her and she leaned against my shoulder. We sat there watching Dad and Grandpa, listening to them still, but I felt better after that. I had my job, I was looking after Mary Jane.

It was growing dark when Mam came down with Miriam.

"We're leaving them two together," said Miriam. "Best thing for them both, and the fever's less."

"Now, Mary Jane," said Mam. "You must get some sleep. Up into our loft you go with Liza."

We passed Mam's bed on the way up and I went to kiss Irene. Mrs Ruswarp was sitting by the bed, holding her hand . . . not talking, just sitting, and Irene was peaceful and resting. I knew then that she would get better, though it might take a long time.

Mam woke us early next morning in her usual brisk way.

She sent Mary Jane down to her mother, for Mrs Ruswarp was preparing to return to her cottage.

"What of Irene?" I asked.

"Irene'll do fine," said Mam.

"But what of the . . . ?"

"The bairn will do fine, so Miriam says, and there's no one better than Miriam for knowing those things. Now, Liza, you're to come with me and fetch the bait."

I stared at Mam. "I'm to go with the flither pickers?"

"Aye, just for today. Irene cannot come and I cannot manage myself, not today."

Mam looked fit to drop. I should have noticed before. She'd have been up in the night looking after Irene, and before that she'd had no sleep for two days and a night.

"I'll go and pick instead of you, Mam."

"Nay, you know nowt about it. Help me for a day or two, then you get yourself off to school. Grandpa says he can see to Billy."

"Must Dad go tonight?"

"Aye he must, if the sea allows, for we've still to eat. We must pick for the Ruswarps too, for their Sam's to go with your dad. He must do the same for Sam as he did for John and poor Mrs Ruswarp must steel herself again."

I wrapped myself up warm and laced on Irene's boots. Lad's boots they were. I fastened her quilted petticoat round me, though I had to tie it with string for her stomach had grown so much bigger than mine.

At last I was to go with the bait gatherers. I was to do the work of a proper fisherman's daughter. I clomped down our stairs, curling my toes at each step for Irene's boots slopped a bit. Mam had Irene's bucket and swill ready and a few extra sacks.

"You'll be needing Irene's mittens," she said.

"Nay, I don't need mittens."

We set off down to the scaur, crossing the bridge, for

the tide had just turned and it still covered the causeway. Other pickers joined us on the way. There were no greetings or halloos as I knew they usually gave, just a nod or a pat and the unspoken knowing that we must get on with our lives and take from the sea as it takes from us.

Mam put out a bucket and a swill for the Ruswarps and the women dropped their contributions in.

And so I set to work, slipping my blunt knife beneath the limpets to break their hold. The first one took three attempts and I caught my thumb, but soon I thought I'd got the knack. Mussels, the finest bait, went into the swill; limpets, which were more plentiful, into the bucket. I picked away for what seemed a long time, my back bent, for it wasn't worth straightening. I began to ache and straightened then, to ease myself. Mam and the others were hard at it and their buckets half-full.

I went back to work, determined to keep up. I picked and picked, but my knife kept slipping and my fingers gathered cuts that stung with the salt water and the juice that oozed from the shellfish. I found that the best flithers were low down where the tide had been, but that was the wettest, most slippery place.

I stopped again to straighten and rest. Aunt Hannah noticed; she would.

"Why lass, we've nobbut started yet."

Mam brought Irene's mittens from her pocket. I took them quick and grateful, pulling them carefully over my sore fingers.

We picked, it seemed, for hours and hours. I felt as though I'd been out on those slippery rocks trying to fill that bucket all my life. I thought I'd never fill it, though it was heavy enough to move, as we went further and further away from our bay.

I slipped into a shallow pool and cursed at my clumsiness, for I'd soaked my thick petticoat that chafed cold and wet against my legs. I was soaked anyway, for an angry rain squall drenched us, and the women picked on.

"I fear we'll be mucking the lines tomorrow," said Hannah. "They'll not be able to get out in this."

"Better to be mucking than having to get that lifeboat out," said Mam.

I could have cried with the weariness of it all. I wondered how we'd managed to get the boat out that night. We'd all been soaked and tired then, but we'd not felt it; warmed by fear, we'd been. The flither picking was quite different. Grim relentless toil, going on and on, and I saw with shame that Mam and even Aunt Hannah were slipping limpets into my bucket as they passed.

I watched Mam's bent back and remembered all the times she'd fought for me to be in school, wanting me to be able to take my chance of something different. I'd have given anything to be in school at that moment.

Still we picked, and I went like one asleep, in a nightmare dream that repeats and repeats, but at last I woke to realise that we were stopping. The women were filling each other's buckets so that we could all return together. They covered the tops with spreading seaweed, for freshness mattered so much.

The walk back was a long weary drag. I was sure my arms were going to break. I kept stopping to rest and getting left behind.

Mam does this every day, I thought, even through the freezing winter months. Ahead of me the others reached the causeway and carried their heavy buckets over, making their short cut. Mam turned away, up round the bay, her usual long way round. I stopped and put my bucket down. Aunt Hannah had waited for me.

"Look," she said pointing. "Just look up there."

Across the causeway, on the top staith, was Grandpa,

with Billy beside him, and a gang of children, all listening to Grandpa's tales.

"Now that's a sight to make you smile," said Hannah. "There's something good come out of that sad night."

I wished it were me up there by Grandpa's side.

"But what of Mam?" I said. "I never thought she'd stick to her long walk back, not after she'd gone out so far, pushing the lifeboat."

"What?" said Hannah. "You thought she'd cross the causeway, did you? Nay Liza Welford, you cannot change a lifetime of fear just like that. Eh, you know nowt lass," and she turned and followed the others, leaving me standing.

I wanted to follow Aunt Hannah, and get home real quick. I dreaded the thought of the shelling and baiting that was still to be done, but that small shape, plodding steadily away from the causeway . . . drew me. I picked up my bucket again and turned Mam's way, shouting her to wait for me.

She stopped, surprised.

"Wait Mam," I shouted. "I want to come your way."

She waited till I came near. "Nay," she said. "You must be daft . . . but then you don't understand."

"I do, Mam," I said. "I do understand. Gran tried to tell me, but she never got it said. So I asked Hannah and I asked Miriam, too. I do know about your little brother William and I'm right sorry about it."

She frowned and bit her lip. I wanted to throw my arms round her and tell her how much I loved her, but I couldn't do that. So I did the only thing I could think to do and I wanted it right enough, what with my aching back and cut fingers.

"Mam," I said. "I *will* go back to school. Not till Irene's better and fit to pick again. But then, I'll go back and I'll work real hard. I will be a pupil teacher, or maybe . . ." I said, thinking of a thin lady, writing at a desk, with no boots for her feet, "maybe I'll do something else."

Mam's rare slow smile warmed me more than sun.

"That's made me glad," she said.

MORE WALKER PAPERBACKS
For You to Enjoy